Little Dog and Duncan

Little Dog and Duncan

Poems by **Kristine O'Connell George**
Illustrated by **June Otani**

Clarion Books ❖ New York

Special thanks to Eva Harris and Regina Gongoll
of Starcrest Kennels, La Tuna, California, and
their champion Irish Wolfhounds.
—J.O.

Clarion Books
a Houghton Mifflin Company imprint
215 Park Avenue South, New York, NY 10003
Text copyright © 2002 by Kristine O'Connell George
Illustrations copyright © 2002 by June Otani

The illustrations were executed in watercolor.
The text was set in 18-point Guardi.

www.houghtonmifflinbooks.com

Printed in Singapore.

Library of Congress Cataloging-in-Publication Data

George, Kristine O'Connell.
Little Dog and Duncan / by Kristine O'Connell George ; illustrated by June Otani.
p.   cm.
ISBN 0-618-11758-X
1. Dogs—Juvenile poetry. 2. Children's poetry, American. [1. Dogs—Poetry. 2. American poetry.]
I. Otani, June, ill. II. Title.
PS3557.E488 L49 2002
811'.54—dc21
2001028481

TWP   10   9   8   7   6   5   4   3   2   1

For Lynne
—K.O.G.

For Caitlyn Kiana and furry friends
Penny, Chibi, and Hektor
—J.O.

Big News

Little Dog yips,
runs in circles,
runs to the door,

barking—

       Visitor!

Hello!

Little Dog and Duncan
touch noses,
wiggle,
wag.

Friend?

Friend!

House Guest

Duncan is coming
to spend the night

bringing special
spend-the-night
Duncan things

in a bag
bigger than
Little Dog.

Homesick

Duncan droops
and mopes
by the front door,
    waiting,
        hoping,
           wanting
to go home.

Little Dog sits close,
helping Duncan mope.

Equality

Duncan gets a hug.
  Little Dog gets a hug.
Duncan gets pats.
  Little Dog gets pats.
Duncan gets a cookie.
  Little Dog gets a cookie.

Fair is fair.

Tactics

Duncan races Little Dog
around the kitchen.

Little Dog slides
under Duncan

     and wins!

Back Door

Little Dog wants out.
Duncan wants in.

Duncan in,
       Little out—

Duncan out,
       Little in—

In.
       Out.

Out.
       In.

Both—
       Out!

No Fair!

Duncan eats
  Little Dog's food.
Duncan drinks
  Little Dog's water.
Part of Duncan is napping
  on Little Dog's bed.

Little Dog is
  miffed.

Crash!

Little Dog and I
run to see

if Duncan
is in

BIG
trouble.

Seating Plan

Half of the backseat
for Little Dog and me,

half for Duncan.

Sit!

Oh, gosh.

Duncan

squashed

the petunias.

19

Fetch!

Little Dog brings a stick

        for me to throw.

Duncan lugs

        half a tree.

No Way!

Little Dog and Duncan
saw me coming
with the brush . . .

The juniper bush
has grown
      a tail.

Mine!

Little Dog hides
all the dog toys
under my bed,

where Duncan
can't fit.

Mine! Mine! Mine!

Little Dog
    sits in my lap,
    faces Duncan
    nose to nose,
    eyeball to eyeball,

and growls:

    This lap is *my* lap.

Walk

Little Dog goes left
and around,
Duncan goes right
and around,

wrapping

all of us

around

and

around

the

lamppost.

27

Grass

Little Dog and Duncan

r o l l

long and slow
in the grass.

So good to roll
with a friend!

Mud

Duncan is a digger.
Little Dog is a digger.

That's how
they met

mud.

Dinner

I fill Little Dog's
          little dog bowl.
I fill Duncan's
          big dog bowl.

Little Dog eats
          Duncan's food.
Duncan eats
          Little Dog's food.

Is Duncan There?

Duncan's family calls
to say good night.

I hold the phone
for Duncan,

who wasn't
expecting
a call.

Scratches

Behind the ears for Little Dog.
Under the chin for Duncan.

Different dogs.
Different itches.
Different scratches.

My Bed

Little Dog
    is supposed to sleep
    in Little Dog's bed.

Duncan
    is supposed to sleep
    in Duncan's bed.

Move over, Little Dog!
Move over, Duncan!

Wishful Thinking

Four eyes begging,
two tails thumping . . .

Thump *thwip* Thump *thwip* Thump *thwip*

A good beat
for bread buttering.

Watchdogs

Duncan and Little Dog
interrupt window watching

to make an announcement—

Yip! Yip! Yip!
Woof! Woof! Woof!

Duncan's family
is coming up the walk!

Going

A goodbye hug
for Duncan
needs to be

v e r y   w i d e.

Gone

Looking out the window,
Little Dog watches
Duncan leave

and whines,

alone.

Still Here?

Duncan is gone.

Little Dog runs
to me to be sure
I'm still here—

and . . .

I am.